little grasshopper books™

Goldilocks and the Three Bears

Get the App!

1. Download the Little Grasshopper Library App* from the App Store or Google Play. Find direct links to store locations at **www.littlegrasshopperbooks.com**

2. Wait for the app to Install and open it.

3. Tap the **+ Add Book** button at the bottom of the screen.**

4. Line up the QR Code Scanner with the QR Code found below.

5. Your book will automatically start downloading to your app!

6. Be sure to accept any prompts that come up.

7. Information on device compatibility and troubleshooting can be found at **www.littlegrasshopperbooks.com**

Based on the classic tale; illustrated by Stacy Peterson.
App content developed in partnership with Filament Games.

Louis Weber, CEO
West Side Publishing, Inc.
8140 Lehigh Avenue
Morton Grove, IL 60053

ISBN: 978-1-64030-903-6
Manufactured in China.
8 7 6 5 4 3 2 1

*We reserve the right to terminate the apps.
**Smartphone not included. Standard data rates may apply to download. Once the app and an individual book's content are downloaded, the app does not use data or require Wi-Fi access.

Once upon a time, Goldilocks went to the meadow to play and pick flowers. But the sun was hot, so she went into the cool, shady forest. She saw a house.

Goldilocks knocked. No one came to the door. She
pushed the door open and went into the house.

Goldilocks was hot and tired. She sat down to wait for the family to come home.

First she sat in the biggest chair. It was too hard!

Next she sat in the middle chair. It was too soft!

Goldilocks sat in the smallest chair. It was just right. But when she rocked back and forth, the chair broke with a big crack! Goldilocks hurried away.

Goldilocks found a kitchen. She saw three bowls of porridge. She was hungry, so she took a bite from the biggest bowl. It was too hot!

Next she took a bite from the medium-sized bowl. It was too cold!

Goldilocks took a bite from the smallest bowl. It was just right! She ate until she had eaten it all!

Goldilocks found the bedroom. She was tired. She said,
"I will take a nap before I walk home."
First she lay down on the biggest bed. It was too hard!

Next Goldilocks tried the middle bed. It was too soft!
Then Goldilocks lay down on the smallest bed. It was
just right! Goldilocks fell asleep.

The three bears came home. They saw right away that someone had been in their house.

"Look! Somebody sat in my chair!" Papa Bear growled.

"And somebody sat in my chair!" Mama Bear said.
"Somebody sat in my chair, too!" Baby Bear squealed.
"And they broke it!"

The bears ran to the kitchen. "Somebody ate some of my porridge!" Papa Bear roared.

"And they ate some of my porridge!" Mama Bear said.

"Somebody ate my porridge, too," Baby Bear squealed. "They ate up every single bite!"

The bears ran to the bedroom next.
"Somebody was in my bed!" Papa Bear roared.
"And somebody was in my bed!" Mama Bear said.

"Look!" Baby Bear squealed. "Somebody is in my bed right now!"

They were all surprised to see a little girl. "What do we do?" Mama Bear asked.

Right then, Goldilocks
woke up.
The bears stared at her.

She stared at the bears.

Before the bears could say anything, Goldilocks tumbled out of bed. She ran away as fast as she could. She never went near the forest again.